Please, Mr. Panda

Por favor, Sr. Panda

A Nan y Frank

Originally published in English in the UK by Hodder Children's Books in 2014 as *Please Mr Panda*

Translated by J.P. Lombana

ISBN 978-0-545-84720-9

10 9 8 7 6 5 4 3 2 15 16 17 18 19/0

Printed in the U.S.A. 08
First Bilingual printing, September 2015

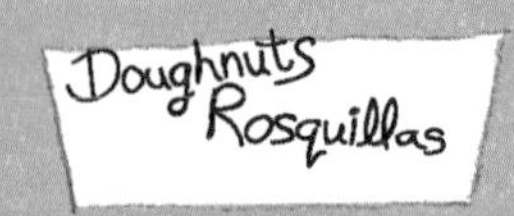

Please, Mr. Panda

Por favor, Sr. Panda

Steve Antony

SCHOLASTIC INC.

Would you like a doughnut?

¿Quieres una rosquilla?

Give me the pink one.

Dame la rosada.

No, you cannot have a doughnut.
I have changed my mind.

No, no te voy a dar una rosquilla.
Me arrepentí.

Would you like a doughnut?

¿Quieres una rosquilla?

I want
the blue one
and
the yellow one.

Quiero
la azul
y
la amarilla.

No, you cannot have a doughnut.
I have changed my mind.

No, no te voy a dar una rosquilla.
Me arrepentí.

Would you like a doughnut?

¿Quieres una rosquilla?

No, go away.

No, vete.

Would you like a doughnut?

¿Quieres una rosquilla?

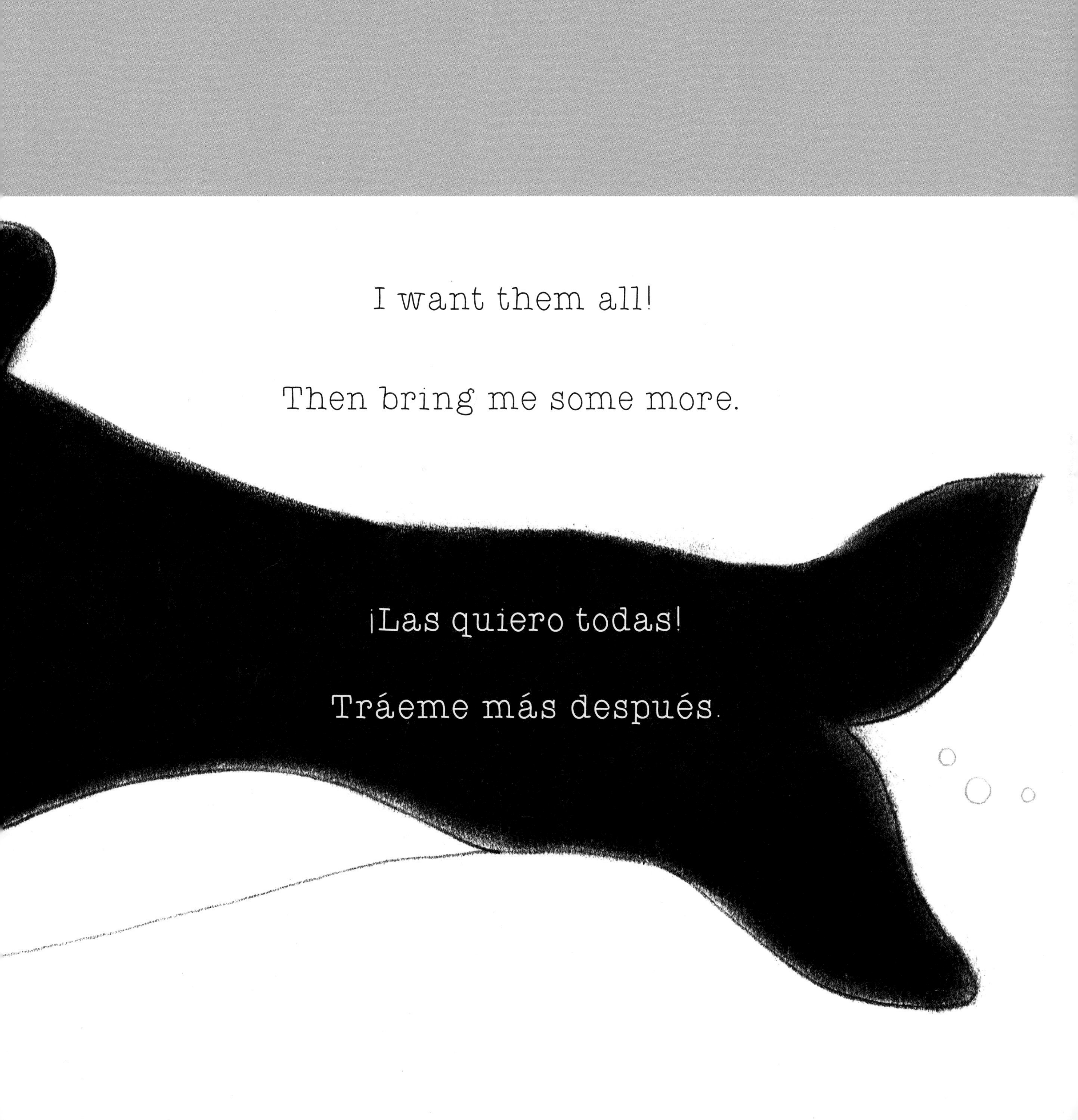

I want them all!

Then bring me some more.

¡Las quiero todas!

Tráeme más después.

No, you cannot have a doughnut.
I have changed my mind.

No, no te voy a dar una rosquilla.
Me arrepentí.

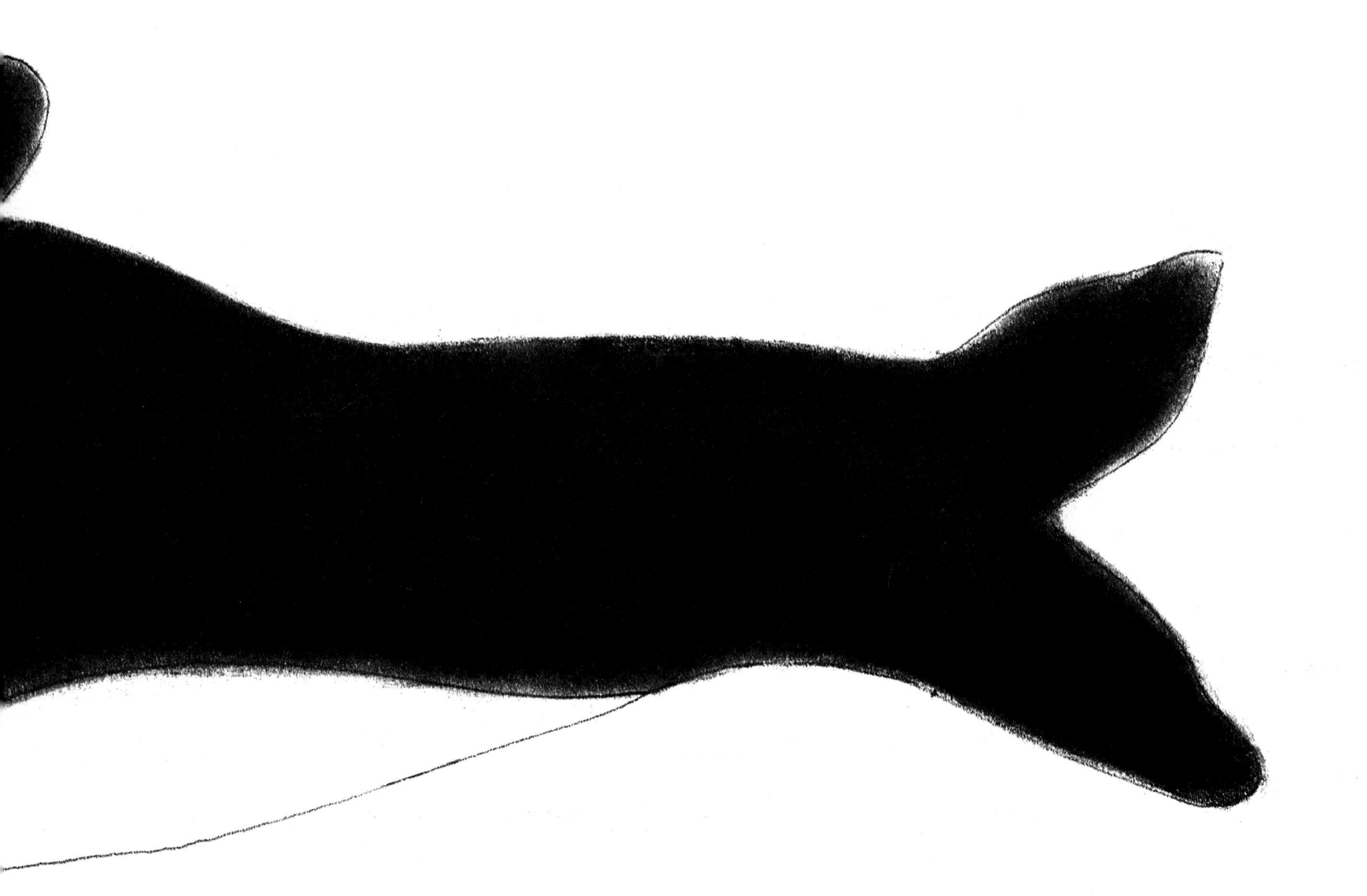

Doughnuts
Rosquillas

Would anyone else like a doughnut?

¿Alguien más quiere una rosquilla?

Doughnuts
Rosquillas

Hello!
May I have a doughnut . . .

¡Hola!
¿Me das una rosquilla...

PLEASE, Mr. Panda?

POR FAVOR, SR. PANDA?

You can have them all.

Te las doy todas.

Thank you very much!

¡Muchas gracias!

Doughnuts
Rosquillas

You're welcome.
I do not like doughnuts.

De nada.
A mí no me gustan.